D0432432

This edition published by Parragon Books Ltd in 2015

Parragon Books Ltd
Chartist House
15–17 Trim Street
Bath BA1 1HA, UK
www.parragon.com

Copyright © 2015 Disney/Pixar.
Materials and characters from the movie Toy Story. Original Disney/Pixar elements © Disney/
Pixar. Slinky® Dog is a registered trademark of Poof-Slinky, Inc. © Poof-Slinky, Inc. All rights
reserved.

ISBN 978-1-4748-0149-2

Printed in China

# Small Fry

Bath • New York • Cologne • Melbourne • Delhi
Hong Kong • Shenzhen • Singapore • Amsterdam

One evening, Bonnie and her mother went to a fast-food restaurant called Poultry Palace for dinner. Bonnie was excited to see which toy would come with her Fun Meal.

But when the cashier gave her the toy, Bonnie frowned.
"A Zurg belt buckle?" she asked the cashier. Bonnie
definitely didn't want a boring belt buckle!

She looked over at the display case, where she saw a mini Buzz Lightyear and a mini Emperor Zurg. "Can I have a Buzz Lightyear instead?"

The cashier shook his head. "I'm sorry. Those are for display only."

Bonnie's mum put an arm round her daughter. "Thanks, anyway. Come on, Bonnie."

BELT BUCKLE

SPACE RANGER

WRIST MISSILE

ZURG COMB

EMPEROR ZURG

BUZZ LIGHTYEAR

LLECT 'EM

BUZZ'S SHIP

In the display case, the mini Buzz watched Bonnie playing in a nearby ball pit with the real Buzz Lightyear and Rex the dinosaur. He nudged the mini Zurg next to him. "I think I just found our ticket to playtime. Let's go!"

Mini Zurg was too nervous to leave. "I don't want to get into trouble with the chicken people," he said.

Mini Buzz wasn't worried about that. He leaped out of the display case and ran to the ball pit. "See ya, Zurgy!"

Mini Buzz waited until Bonnie wasn't looking before he made his move. He sneaked up behind the real Buzz, then he quickly pushed him deep beneath the colourful balls.

Mini Buzz popped up next to Rex and glanced over at the dinosaur. "Playtime's the best!"

Soon it was time to go home. Bonnie's mum grabbed
Rex and Mini Buzz and put them in Bonnie's backpack.
Mini Buzz was thrilled. His plan was working! Bonnie's
mum hadn't noticed that he wasn't the real Buzz!

Later that night, the real Buzz Lightyear finally crawled out of the ball pit and realized he was trapped inside Poultry Palace! As he tried to escape, he fell through a loose grate – and landed in a circle of strange toys.

A mermaid toy spoke first. "Well, hello! Welcome to the support group for discarded Fun Meal toys."

Buzz looked around. He was very confused. "Uh, I think there's been a mistake. You see, I was just left in the ball pit."

The mermaid turned toward Buzz. "Oh, we've all been left in the ball pit of life, haven't we?"

Before Buzz could answer, she continued. "Let's go around the room and introduce ourselves. My name is Neptuna."

"Hi, Neptuna," the toys replied in unison.

Next came a steak robot toy. "I'm T-Bone, leader of the Steak Force. I, uh, well ... I never got played with."

One by one, all the other toys in the circle introduced themselves to Buzz. He knew he needed to get back to his friends, but how would he escape?

Meanwhile, in Bonnie's bedroom, Rex and Mini Buzz hopped out of Bonnie's backpack.

Mini Buzz greeted the other toys. "I'm Buzz Lightyear. I come in peace!"

Jessie wasn't fooled at all. "What happened to Buzz?"

Rex tried to explain. "He says the plastic in the ball pit made him shrink."

Mini Buzz agreed. "Yeah, yeah, that's right, Tex."

"Where's the real Buzz?" asked Woody, unconvinced. But Mini Buzz had no interest in revealing his true identity. He was having too much fun! He grabbed Woody's hat and ran around the room!

"It's playtime! I'll be the cowboy!" he yelled.

That was the last straw. The toys tackled Mini Buzz and tied him to a glue bottle. The little toy confessed that he had left Buzz behind at Poultry Palace.

He tried to talk his way out of trouble by getting Jessie on his side. "So, uh … I used to work at Poultry Palace. You like honey mustard sauce?"

Jessie just crossed her arms and sighed. She hoped Woody would come up with a plan – and soon!

Back inside Poultry Palace, Buzz was making a plan
of his own. He knew the only way out was through an
open ceiling vent. But how could he get up there?
Then Buzz noticed a toy named Gary Grappling Hook.

"Gary, do you mind?"

He aimed Gary at the vent above them. The toy shot
up and hooked himself onto the vent, pulling Buzz up,
up, up and out of sight!

In Bonnie's bedroom, the toys gathered round a map of Poultry Palace.

Woody took charge. "Okay, to save Buzz, we need to find a way to get inside Poultry Palace."

Hamm suggested picking the lock. One of the toys wanted to drive a truck right through the front door!

"Or you could use the drive-thru," came a new voice. It was Buzz! He was back!

After Buzz greeted his friends, he walked over to Mini Buzz and glared at the tiny toy. "So, what do you have to say for yourself, Space Ranger?"

Mini Buzz just gulped.

Later at Poultry Palace, Mini Buzz apologized to Buzz with
the help of the unwanted toys. "I've spent a lot of playtime
thinking I was the prize that came with the meal. I know now
that the real prize is what's inside each and every one of us!"

The other toys applauded, and Buzz rested his hand
on Mini Buzz's shoulder. It looked like Mini Buzz had finally
found somewhere he could fit in.